KT-500-134

OPEN VERY CAREFULLY

C0000 020 129 712

For Dylan, Sam and Alex
N.B.
For my Mum and Dad, who have always supported me
while letting me think I was doing it all by myself.
N.O.

OPEN VERY

First published in 2013 by Nosy Crow Ltd
The Crow's Nest, 10a Lant Street,
London SE1 1QR
www.nosycrow.com

ISBN 978 0 85763 084 1 (PB)

Nosy Crow and associated logos are trademarks
and /or registered trademarks of Nosy Crow Ltd.

Text Copyright © Nosy Crow 2013
Illustrations copyright © Nicola O'Byrne 2013

The right of Nicola O'Byrne to be identified as the
illustrator of this work has been asserted.

All rights reserved

This book is sold subject to the condition that it shall not, by way of trade or otherwise, be lent,
hired out or otherwise circulated in any form of binding or cover other than that in which
it is published. No part of this publication may be reproduced, stored in a retrieval system,
or transmitted in any form or by any means (electronic, mechanical, photocopying,
recording or otherwise) without the prior written permission of Nosy Crow Ltd.

A CIP catalogue record for this book is available from the British Library.

Printed in Italy by Imago

9 8 (PB)

~~The Ugly Duckling~~ CAREFULLY

~~Hans Christian Andersen~~

Nicola O'Byrne

With words by Nick Bromley

nosy crow

Once upon a time, there was a mother duck with three pretty ducklings and one . . .

Wait a minute!

What's that?

I'm trying to read you the story of The Ugly Duckling, but there's something in this book that shouldn't be here!

Do you **dare** to keep looking?

You do?

Then let's turn the page **very, very** carefully . . .

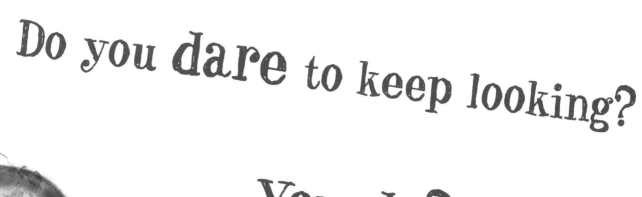

It's a . . .

. . . CROCODILE!

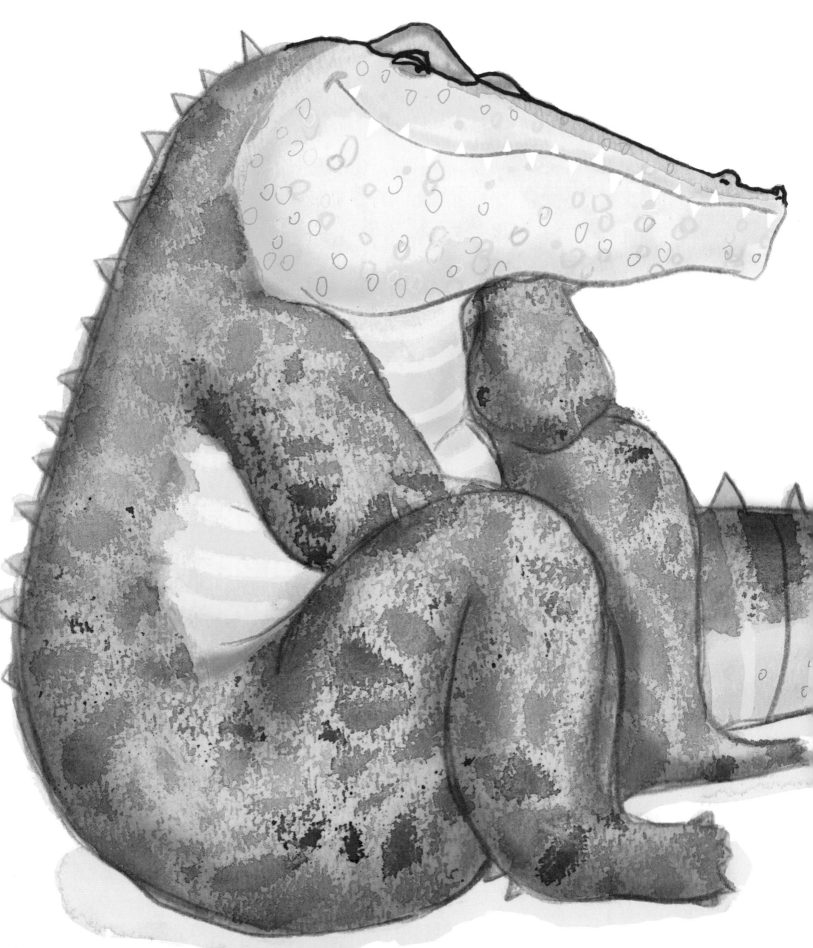

A really big scary one!

What's he doing in
this book?

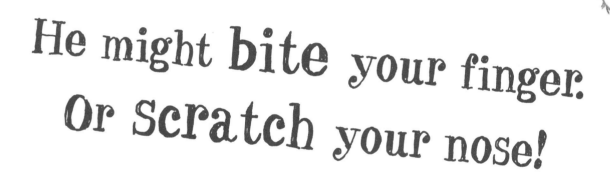

He might **bite** your finger.
Or **scratch** your nose!

I've heard crocodiles
like to do that.
Stay back
just in case . . .

Watch out!
He's on the move.

What is he doing?

He's eating the letters!

He must be **hungry!**

I think his favourite letters to eat are O and S.

St p!

Mr Cr c dile!

Y u can't eat the letter !

Now he's gobbling up . . .

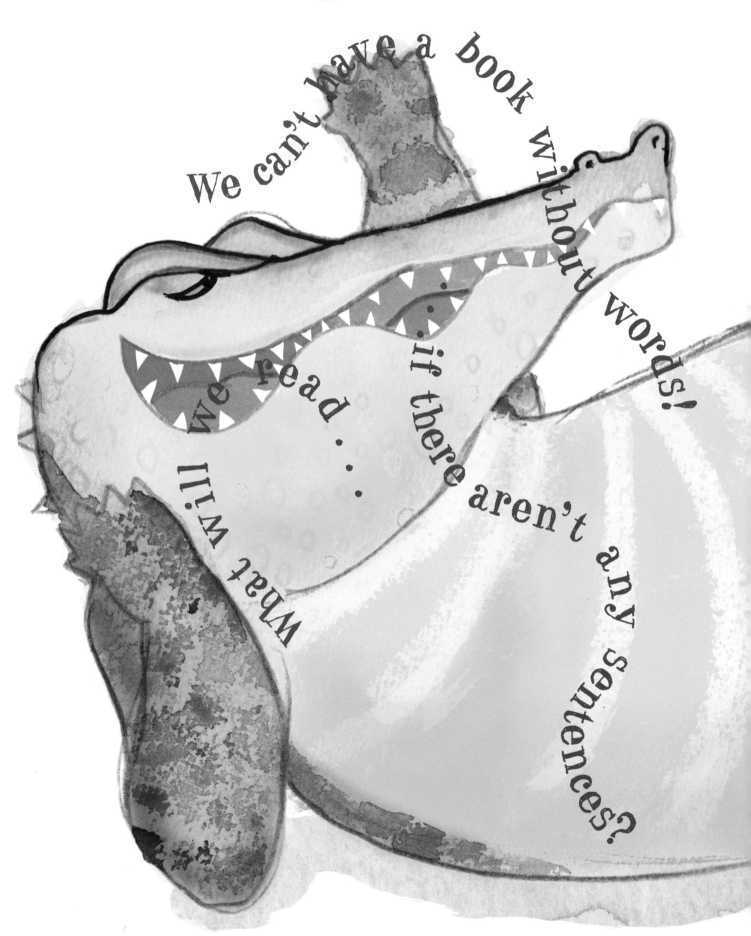

We can't have a book without words!

What will we read . . . . . if there aren't any sentences?

...whole words
and
SENTENCES!

We've got to make him stop....

Let's try
rocking
the book
backwards

and

 **forwards.**

That's it . . .

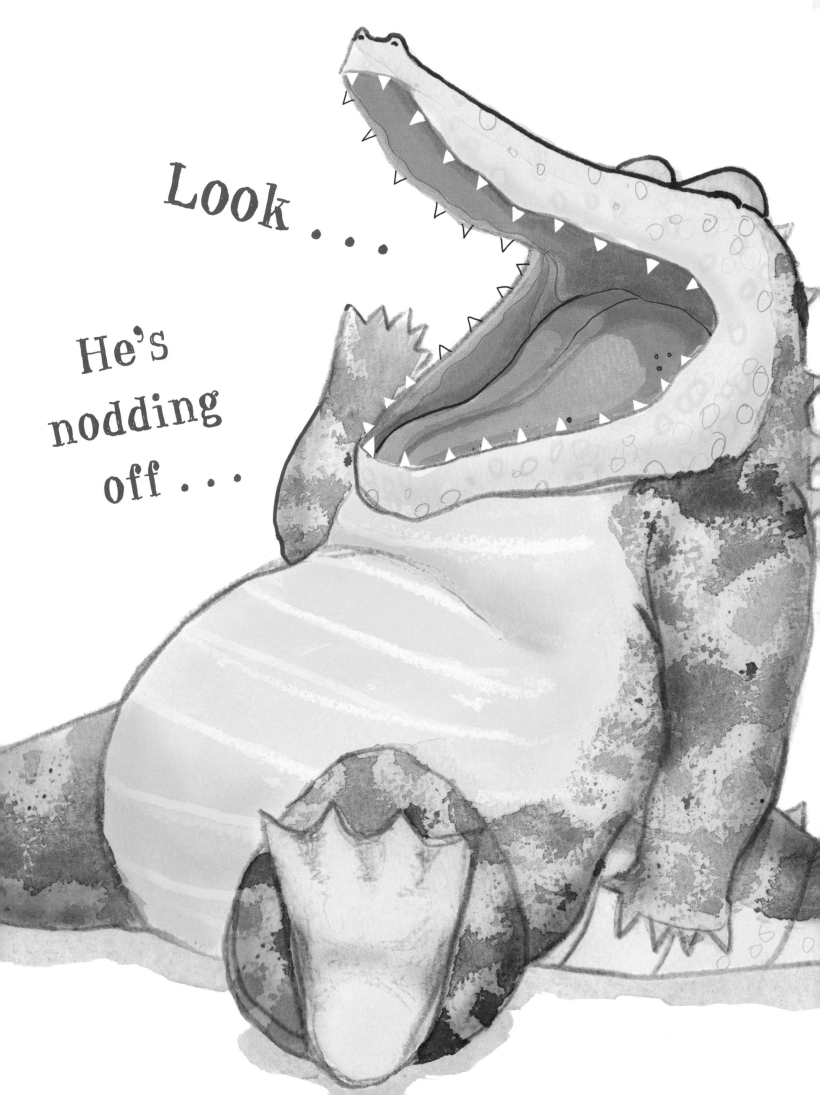

Look . . .

He's
nodding
off . . .

A A A HH . . .

He's sleeping like a baby.

I know . . .

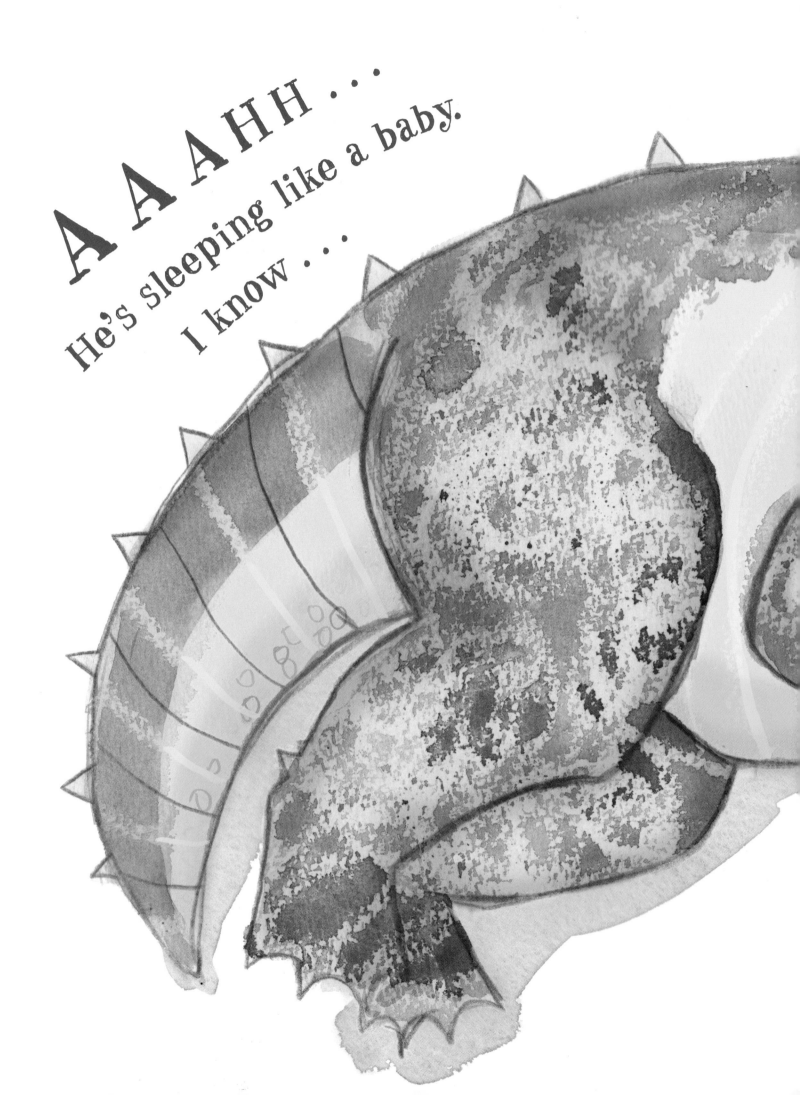

. . . let's find a crayon.
If you're going to eat our words,
Mr Crocodile, then we're going to draw on you!

SSSHHH...

He's not such a scary

crocodile now!

Maybe he **is** a
scary crocodile after all!
All that drawing has
woken him up!

And he's not looking too happy
about that tutu.
Crocodiles don't do ballet!

Watch out!

It looks as if he's had enough of this book . . .

I think he's
going to make a
run for it!

Here
he
goes . . .

Ouch!

Well, who would
have thought it was so hard
to get out of a book?

Maybe if you
Shake
the book,
he'll
fall
out.

Hmm. That didn't work either.
But look!

He's worked out
what to do.

He's
munching
a hole
through
the page.

And he is nearly out!

Goodbye, Mr Crocodile!

I wasn't scared.
Were you?

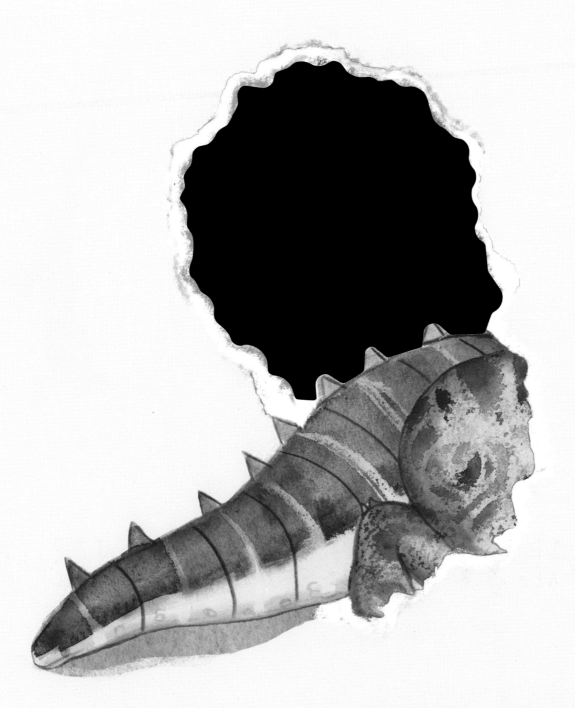

I wonder where he'll
turn up next?